THE BEAR

Library of Congress Cataloging in Publication Data

Steiner, Jörg.   The bear who wanted to be a bear.
Translation of Der Baer der ein Baer bleiben wollte.
[1. Bears—Fiction] I. Müller, Jörg. II. Title.
PZ7.S8262Be [E] 76-29355
ISBN 0-689-50079-3

From an idea by
Frank Tashlin
adapted by
Jörg Steiner

Illustrated by
Jörg Müller

WHO WANTED TO BE A BEAR

A Margaret K. McElderry Book

Atheneum New York

Leaves were falling from the trees. Flocks of wild geese, high above, were flying south. A brown bear felt the cool wind ruffle his fur. He was feeling very sleepy.

It smells of snow, he thought, as he scuffed through the rustling leaves on the way to his favorite den.

Soon he was fast asleep. Like all bears, he would sleep through winter. Outside his den, the wind rushed through the woods. It began to snow. Winter had come, and the bear slept on.

Then something unusual happened. Along with winter came a lot of men. They brought blueprints and tools with them and they cut down all the trees—tree after tree after tree.

The men brought in machines and cranes and began to build a factory, right in the middle of the forest. They came in truckloads through the snowy wilderness. The ground was frozen so hard that even the heavy bulldozers didn't sink in.

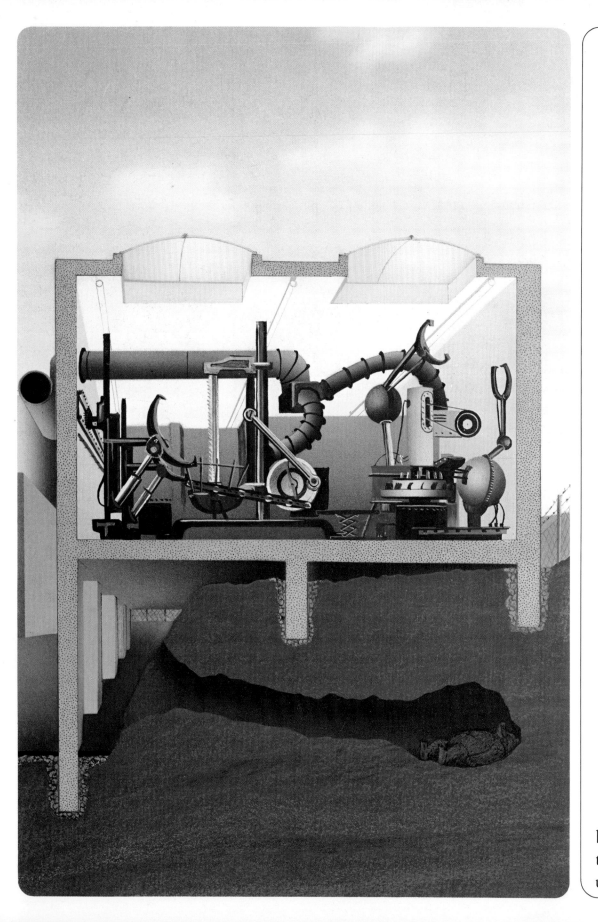

When spring arrived at last, the bear woke up, deep down under the ground. It is not easy to get up after such a long sleep.

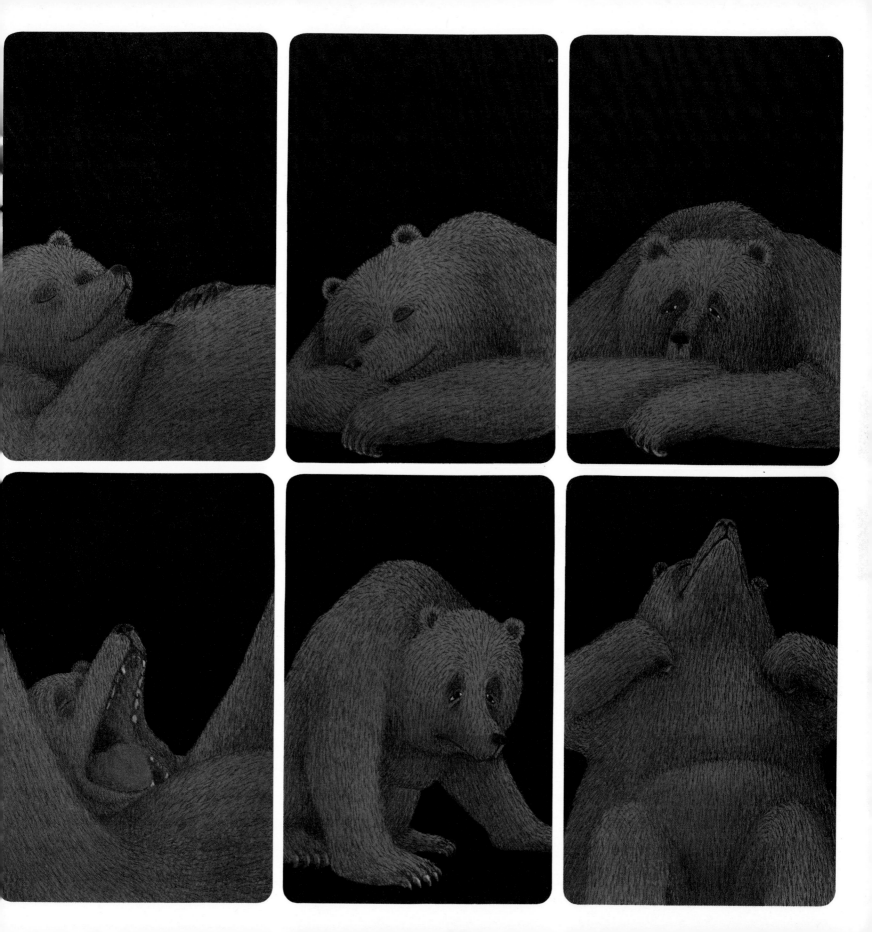

The bear yawned and stretched. Then he crawled to the front of his den.

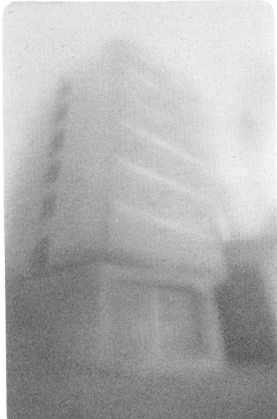

He was blinded by the bright light. I must still be asleep, he thought, and rubbed his eyes. But no, what he had seen was real. The forest had disappeared.

The bear could only stand and stare at the factory. And while he was staring, a factory guard came running up to him.

"Hey, you, get to work!" the guard yelled.

The bear felt his heart leap into his throat.

"Excuse me," he said politely, "but I am a bear."

"A bear!" the guard shouted. "Don't make me laugh! You're a no-good lazybones!"

The guard was so angry that he took the bear to the Personnel Manager.

"I am a bear," the bear said again, very politely. "You must be able to see that."

"What I see is my business!" the Personnel Manager roared.

"And I don't see a bear; I see a dirty, unshaven lazybones!"

And the Personnel Manager took the bear to the Vice-President.

The Vice-President had already heard the story and he was very angry too.

When the bear entered the room, the Vice-President was talking on the phone to the Director. "We've got a lazy worker here," he said. "The man claims he is a bear. Just imagine, a bear! I know your time is precious, but I think you should take a look at this unshaven lazybones."

The Director didn't waste much time with the bear. He didn't shout, he didn't roar, he only glanced up from his newspaper and said, "A dirty character. Take him to the President! He's waiting for him."

The President was the most powerful man in the factory. He earned more money than all the others, and he had the biggest office. But he did not have much to do and was often bored. So he listened quietly to the bear. He had plenty of time and he was glad of the change.

"Well, well," he said. "So you're a bear?"

"Yes," the bear said. "I'm glad I have found someone who believes me."

"Wait," the President said. "I didn't say that. If you're really a bear, you'll have to prove it to me."

"Prove it?" the bear asked.

"That's right," said the President. "There are real bears at the zoo and in the circus. They will know if you are telling the truth or not."

So the President in his limousine and the bear in a bus were driven a long way to the nearest town with a zoo. The bears at the zoo shook their heads when they saw the unfamiliar bear climbing out of the bus.

"You're not a real bear," they said. "A real bear doesn't drive around in a bus. A real bear lives behind bars, just like we do."

"Or in a bear pit," said an old bear who had spent many years of his life in a bear pit.

"That's not true!" the forest bear cried out angrily. "I am a bear! I am a bear!"

"Most of all, you're stubborn," the President said and smiled.

"But we'll have to find out who's right. There's a circus in the next large city. We'll drive there."

And so they did. Circus bears are considered to be very intelligent, since they've learned everything they know from human beings.

The circus bears took a long look at the unfamiliar bear.

"He looks like a bear," they finally said. "But he isn't a bear. A bear doesn't sit in the audience. A bear dances. Can you dance?"

"No," the bear said, unhappily.

"You see what I mean!" the smallest circus bear exclaimed.

"He can't even dance! He's nothing but an unshaven lazybones with his lazy bones in a fur coat."

They all laughed, the President as well. The bear, however, felt so sad and afraid, he didn't know what to do.

But I am sure of it, he thought to himself during the long trip back to the factory. I *know* I'm a bear. Why don't the others know it? I *know* I'm a bear.

When he was given overalls in the factory, however, he didn't resist.

He shaved himself when he was ordered to shave.

He punched his card in the time clock just like all the other workers. And then he was assigned a place at a machine. The guard told him what he was supposed to do and the bear nodded, although he hadn't understood a word. He stood perplexed in front of the big control board. The other workers seemed to know exactly what was expected of them. They were pressing different buttons.

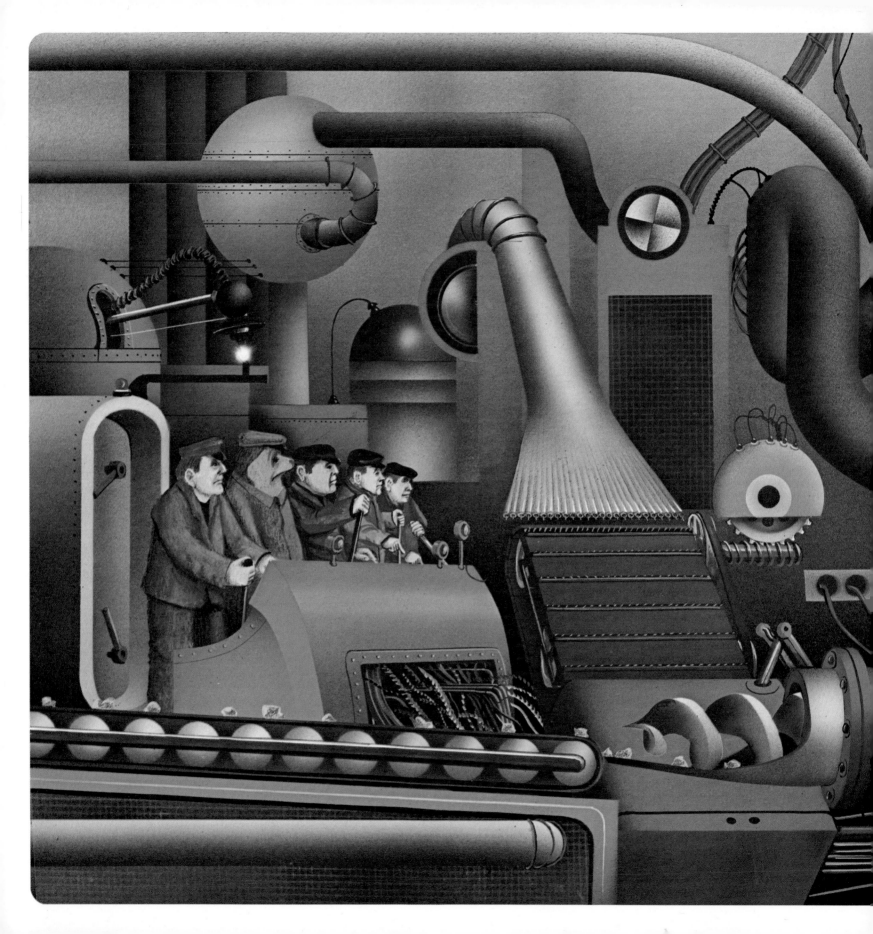

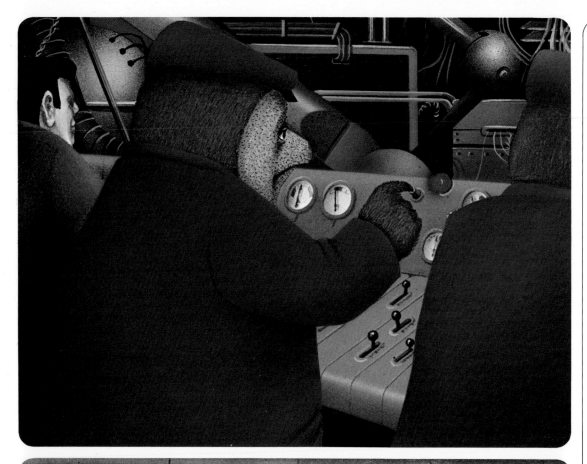

When the factory guard turned up again, the bear quickly touched a button. Nothing happened.

"Hey, you," the guard yelled. "Are you going to get started pretty soon?"

The bear reached out again and pressed the button firmly. The machine didn't groan and moan, it didn't explode. Only a red light lit up and went out again.

The bear had become a factory worker. Every day he stood at the machine along with the other workers.

Lilies of the valley bloomed in the meadow outside the high factory fence and wilted away again. Then the summer heat dried out the grasses, and the bear often lay awake during the warm, bright August nights. Violent storms came, and when the storms were gone, autumn arrived. During the noon break one day, the bear stood and watched the wild geese drawn out in a long line across the sky.

"Bet you're dreaming again, you old bum!" the guard yelled at him.

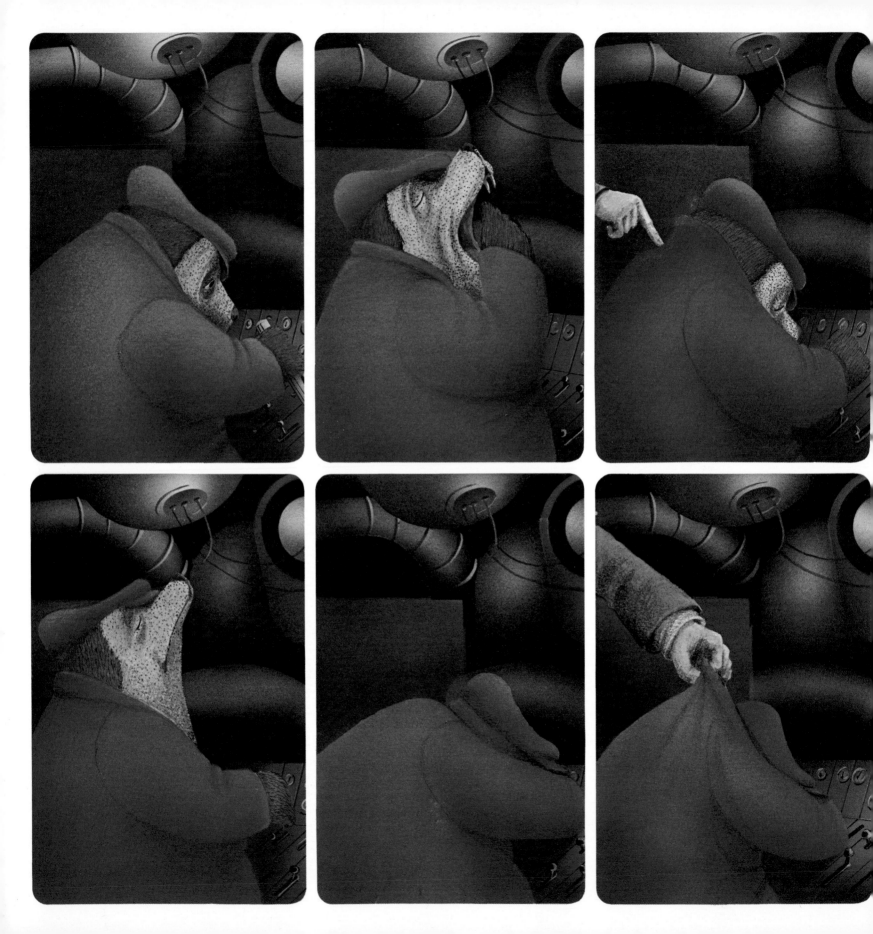

The more brightly colored the leaves on the trees became, the sleepier grew the bear. The harder the leaves danced in the autumn wind, the sleepier grew the bear. It smells of snow, he thought to himself, and I am very tired. Each morning the other workers had to pull him out of bed, and he kept falling asleep at the machine, too.

One day the guard came running up. "You're ruining the whole job," he shouted. "We can't use a lazy-bones like you here any more. Get out—you're fired!"

The bear stared at him. "Fired?" he asked. "Does that mean that I can go wherever I want to? And nobody will try to stop me?"

"Get out right away!" the guard roared. "And don't ever stick your nose in here again, get it?"

The bear didn't wait to hear that twice. He fetched his bundle of belongings and got going.

For a day and a whole night and the next day, the bear walked along the shoulder of the highway, for there were no other roads to follow.

He counted the cars that drove by, but in the factory he had only learned to count to five, so he finally gave up. It began to snow harder and harder.

At dusk of the second day, wet and cold, he reached the only motel in many miles.

Though the desk clerk didn't have anything to do, he tried to look terribly busy, and he let the bear wait for quite some time before asking what he wanted.

"I'm very tired," the bear answered politely. "I'd like a room."

"Well, well, a room," the desk clerk said and took a good look at the bear. "But we never rent a room to a worker—and certainly not to a bear!"

"What?" the bear asked.

"I said we never rent a room to a worker—and certainly not to a bear!"

"Did you say 'bear'?" the bear asked. "Does that mean you think *I* could be a bear?"

The desk clerk reached for the telephone to call the manager. But that wasn't necessary. The bear had already gone out and had shut the door behind him.

He trudged slowly through the snow, on his way to the forest.

He didn't really know why he was going there, but he went on and on, until at last he reached a den.

"I must think about all of this," the bear said to himself, and he sat down in front of the den. "If only I weren't so terribly tired. But I must think this over." He thought and he yawned.

He sat there for a long time, staring into space, listening to the wind in the trees, letting the snow cover him.

"I feel as if I've forgotten something important. What can it be?"

Then he remembered.